Otis

JANIE BYNUM

HARCOURT, INC.

San Diego   New York   London

Printed in Hong Kong

Otis was a very fine pig.
He had soft, silky hairs
and pink, pink skin.

How such a neat pig was
born to such a sloppy family
was anyone's guess.

When his brothers played rugby in the swamp, Otis kept score on the sidelines.

When his sisters played tag in the wallow, Otis counted buttercups in the grass.

Otis tried very hard
to remain a spotless pig.

But making friends wasn't easy.

His mama told him, "Someday, Otis, you will like the mud."

And Otis replied, "Oh, Mama, I don't think so."

Otis imagined mud oozing around his hooves, making a
sticky, sucking noise as he lifted one foot, then the other.

He imagined mud drying on his skin, leaving dirty patches all over his pink, pink body.

Even when he did his chores,
Otis managed to stay clean.

While his brothers weeded the
corn, Otis hauled the weeds away,
careful not to get a spot of mud
on his pink, pink self.

While his sisters picked the ripe corn,
Otis sorted the good ears from the bad,
making sure not a bit of dirt soiled him.

Otis was lonely.
All the other pigs
loved mud.

But no matter how
hard he tried, he just
couldn't stand the stuff.

His papa told him, "Someday, Otis, you will like the mud."

And Otis replied, "Oh, Papa, I don't think so."

One day as Otis returned
from the garden, he heard
a small, croaky sob.

There by the wallow
sat a little frog,
crying softly.

"Little Frog, why are you crying?" Otis asked.

"I've lost my favorite ball in the middle of the mud," Little Frog said.

"Well, that's not so bad. Go get it," Otis said.

"But I can't cross the mud!" Little Frog wailed.

"Why not?" Otis asked. "Frogs love mud and all things swampy."

"Not *this* frog!" Little Frog cried. "Please wade in and get my ball," he begged. "Pigs love mud and all things sloppy."

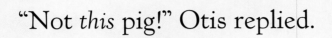
"Not *this* pig!" Otis replied.

Little Frog stopped crying, and croaked a little laugh.
Otis oinked a little giggle.

"I have an idea," Otis said. "I'll hold on to this branch, and you can hop out to get your ball."

"That's a fine idea," Little Frog said.

And that is what they did.

The rest of the afternoon, Otis and
Little Frog tossed the ball back
and forth on the nice, clean grass.

And from that day on, the two
friends played together everywhere—
except, of course . . .

. . . in the mud.

To Linda S.—
for your friendship and inspiration

Library of Congress Cataloging-in-Publication Data
Bynum, Janie.
Otis/by Janie Bynum.
p.   cm.
Summary: Because he doesn't like the mud, Otis is different
from the other pigs and has trouble finding friends.
[1. Individuality—Fiction.   2. Pigs—Fiction.   3. Cleanliness—Fiction.
4. Friendship—Fiction.   5. Frogs—Fiction.]   I. Title.
PZ7.B9888Ot   2000
[E]—dc21   99-6087
ISBN 0-15-202153-1

First edition
A C E G H F D B

The illustrations in this book were done in pen-and-ink and watercolor
on Fabriano soft-press watercolor paper.
The display type was hand-lettered by Janie Bynum.
The text type was set in Kennerly.
Color separations by Bright Arts Ltd., Hong Kong
Printed by South China Printing Company, Hong Kong
This book was printed on totally chlorine-free Nymolla Matte Art paper.
Production supervision by Stanley Redfern and Ginger Boyer
Designed by Linda Lockowitz